Black Harlequin

The Romance Revealed

Storm

BOOK NINE

Contents

Preface

In the enchanting realm of secreted desires, playful fantasies and foreign escapades that break

the ice for lovers, there can be drama where love and passion that is undulated like the gentle

rhythms of a symphony daring to hold open the return of possibilities. Time spent in lover's

embrace is disrupted by a clandestine plot which unfolds deep within the shadows.

Queel, a mysterious and enigmatic figure, held the key to a grand plan that would ignite

forbidden desires and alter the course of romance in Book 9 of Black Harlequin The Romance

Revealed book series.

As the curtains rose on this tale of forbidden love, readers were introduced to the alluring yet

treacherous world of Queel. With every step he took, his intentions remained shrouded in

secrecy leaving a masquerade for those around him entranced by his enigma. But little did they

know that Queel's true weapon of seduction lay not in his charm or charisma, but in the secrets

he held and the plots he carefully orchestrated..

With the stage set for an epic romance, Queel devised a cunning plan, intertwining the threads

of love and deception. His unexpected prelude to romance captivated Astyarress' soul from the

beginning, for he had prepared not just romance but persuasion for a menu of unexpected

poetry that sets bodies in motion.

As the lovers move towards a fate they never could have imagined there's only more to reveal.

But Queel was not just a master of sweet nothings whispered behind closed doors.

Troubled whispers escaped his lips like ripples in a wave, teasing and tempting to borderline in

the lives of those surrounding him and dared listen.

They carried with them a dangerous undercurrent that threatened to disrupt the harmony

Queel had so meticulously crafted. As these ripples reverberated throughout Astyarress, they

unleashed a wave of reminiscence that proved to be both captivating and distracting.

Caught up in his own masterpiece, Queel found himself hesitating at the crucial moment of his

exit. The hesitation was like a crack in a mirror, threatening to shatter the illusion he had created. This distraction became the undoing of his carefully laid plans, as the secrets he had guarded so fiercely threatened to spill into the open.

As the water in this cauldron of desire reached its boiling point, the truth began to seep through the cracks. Queel's grand plan, his masterstroke, was about to take center stage. Astyarress held to her confidence, hoping that the revelation

of her performance and pleasurable nights, now hidden abroad from the circle of friends who entrusted her based upon her assets, would remain hidden investments.

Forever would change the landscape and direction of her life as she continues to seek riches untold.

Months in the making, Black Harlequin: The Romance Revealed promised to be a literary masterpiece, unraveling the intricate tapestry of love, passion,and deception. As each page turned, it revealed more sides to the story, peeling back the layers of secrets and unveiling the truth that had been unknowingly concealed. Readers are left with some unforgettable poetry accompanied with some unforgettable love scenes as Queel comes out of the shadows.

Amongst the tumultuous sea of desire and intrigue, the fate of Astyarress becomes her steps into not only some new attire but she'll be wearing those tattoos branded by her lovers stain.

 Would Queel's machinations crush everything in its path, including Astyarress' beloved Drippe?

Or would love triumph over the darkness, lighting a path towards redemption?

The readers eagerly awaited the publication of Book 9, knowing that within its pages lay an epic tale that would challenge their hearts and minds. For within this story, entwined with the words of clever characters, lie the secrets and revelations that would forever change their perception of romance - a truth waiting to be uncovered in Black Harlequin: The Romance Revealed.

I feel.
As you do.
I touch
It's your VooDoo
Still wearing you
I feel.
As you do.
Can't breathe
Without you.
As you do.
I feel
If it's all of you
I was apart of it too
If it wasn't
As you do
Without you
It couldn't
Last
I feel.
As you do
Lay down
As you do.
Breathe
As you do.
Touch
As you do.
I feel.
As You do.
Caress me
As you do.
All of you.
Call me
Feel me As you do   - Jocelyn

Chapter One

Queel

Queel's entanglement into this sorted blackmail turned pass around whoe, oversea show or whoe down had been several months into the making. In fact the months had turned into just about two years with the fashion show campaign coming to its surprising close.

The red curtains had come down and closed on the blackmail streaming, but not before the footage had surmounted enough to give a lil excitement to Queel who had been eagerly waiting to cash in on his home studio porn, xnae the volunteerism.

What had been love between the sheets, a bold stray right in front of everyone, but no one had spoken about it, especially to Ebony's lady, Emystary. But was it the revenue that was flowing in with this year's fashion show campaign, Ebony had benefited well financially despite the whirlwind he'd gotten caught up in.

Queel had set his sights on Emystary becoming more than a cash cow, but he had plans to ease into Emystary's bed in Ebony's absence only too soon had the footage gotten a lil bit hotter than expected before the wine could chill on any night he would set for Emystary. On his better days, better yet not the transparent thief behind the camera lens. Stolen were those moments the three of them whispered between glances, separate but they all knew how in depth the affair had become, leaving nothing else to the imagination.

Pharaoh had brought the heat alright and now it was time to end the sneaky trailblazing of Queel. If Emystary found out sooner than later it might affect some dividends becoming in error of allocation as Queel saw it. Or was it sincerity and hushed because no one, if anyone was to come forth with any "showtime" incidents it would hurt Emystary. The love romance had unfolded over the cusps of their intimate lives into the social sectors.

Queel would have to answer for his deceitful ploy and he contemplated for a moment about Astyarress. Queel and Astyarress had come along way together, their past, the get rich schemes slash occupational survivor jobs slash lover's entanglement without hearts to care about the consequences of sexual escapades along the way. It was a now too far along not to be a do or die endeavor. Unbeknownst to Queel, the hustle was not going to produce the flow he wanted.

Astyarress was primo, an exemplification of what exactly that meant. Damn did she not just sex three men along the way to a fashion model career slash lover to a wealthy man? All within say about a year's time. Who had been the better charmer or had Astyarress been being P.I.M.P-ed out while enjoying leaving causalities along the way. Queel was even more of a client case study with his obvious 3D, interactive porn and episodic stages in which his progressed into his next moves.

Astyarress had been cast and playing her role as a seductress and side piece whilst meanwhile, Ebony, a picture-perfect epitome of loyalty, played his role with such conviction that even the gods themselves would have been fooled. Bound by an unfaltering love for Emystary, he painted a portrait of devotion so convincing that only the whispering wind carried the truth of his clandestine trysts with Astyarress. Ebony had been putting on his best role as the faithful lover to Emystary.

Queel had only the most to conceal, seeing everything from behind the camera, the screen and participating as director, producer, editor and writer of this masterplan, his blueprints to become yet a wealthier man than both Ebony, Lotus and Pharaoh.

Had it really been fools gold?

Queel had been planning on making a Copperfield exit after cashing in on his blackmail schemes. He and Astyarress had been in a long term open relationship in the past, as in their porn careers, but this time it was different with Ebony. Queel had watched Ebony and Emystary for some time now and he had hoped to have slept with Emystary by now, but that didn't go as planned in his affairs of deceitful games. Queel had acquired a secreted lover himself throughout the months during which time he was coaching Astyarress. Another "P" (pussy) in the recipe so to speak had a lure that beckoned Queel to end things with Astyarress aside from what he had been viewing, the affair, the seduction and the sex between Astyarress and Ebony as he kept quiet.

With a mischievous glint in his eyes, Queel orchestrated a tantalizing web of desire and deceit, his puppet strings extending far and wide. Astyarress, a vixen of unimaginable allure, effortlessly commanded the attention of every eye that fell upon her, her seductive prowess unmatched by any mortal soul. And yet, she was but a pawn in Queel's grand scheme, a tempting side piece in his intricate tableau.

Oh, the pleasure he derived

from the forbidden fruit,

the intoxication of secrets

buried beneath sheets of passion...

But behind the scenes, Queel, the enigmatic mastermind, reveled in the shadows, orchestrating a symphony of desire and manipulation. His razor-sharp mind, like a sculptor's chisel, carefully crafted each moment, caught each stolen glance, and pulled the strings of their lives as if they were mere marionettes in his twisted game.

Through carefully chosen camera angles and meticulously penned words his puppet Astyarress had planted, Queel had succeeded in his trap he'd laid for Ebony and Emystary, his ascent to untold riches and power if accomplished.

At least for a little while.

From the confines of his surveillance-filled home studio, Queel observed Ebony in the studio, as well as from a distance, envisioning a foundation that would ensure his own security.

Over the years, Queel had maintained control over Astyarress through his persuasive nature, dominance, and ability to fulfill her desires beyond mere physical intimacy, especially in answering her appetite in many more ways than just sexing her the way she wanted it over the years. Queel did know Astyarress, but the demons circling the new creatures in the shadows of their day-lit lives had been eating away at the long term pack he and Astyarress had come to know and trust in one another.

Yet, lurking within the depths of Queel's heart, a secret burned bright, a secret lover who quietly colluded with him in their web of passion and betrayal. It was a forbidden love, concealed from prying eyes, a clandestine affair that whispered promises of ecstasy in the moonlit hours. Like a mystical siren, this mysterious presence seduced Queel away from Astyarress, entangling him further in this web of deceit. One minute he was gathering footage, coaching Astyarress, who knew exactly what to do and how much room to give Queel who was not only watching her have sex with someone else, Queel still remained his coy self, and rather humored by getting some pussy himself through the whole affair. No one had questioned Queel as to who he was in the bed with night after night, while the couples played sheepishly with one another, even Astyarress had some honeymooner days alone with Ebony as if he were entirely her man. A fantasy she had been skating on ice with, while melting this handsome, chiseled man right down to his bare skin. More than a candle in the wind to burn. Burning were the nights in Mansura as Ebony and Astyarress brought a behind the scenes set of their own. Two models turned pro actors.

As the affair between Astyarress and Ebony had been flaunted upon the stage, yet secreted, Queel watched, he felt his heart torn this time, between the desire for riches and casting off Astyarress, which is what he had come to realize rather than what was to be a get away. Their ship had sailed. This would be their last time working together and he hoped that they both would prosper, more so he didn't want the blueprints of his plan to fall apart. He would continue the fasode at home around the studio.

Although the sands of time had slipped through his fingers slowly, he had gotten impatient over the months while Astyarress was lacing her pockets funded by Emystary and Ebony's lucrative business partnership, while his salary remained mediocre. He was fasting off prospective outcomes of his lover's newly cast acting career in the bedroom. "Hussie by night and scandalous by day", as Queel said to himself. He saw it for what it really was, he knew what it was, and he had agreed to the whole "sham-lot" plot. As if he was on some porn set, not equally gratified with pay, but he was watching his longtime lover fuck another man's brains out every chance she could motivated by a payoff he'd set-up. "Damn I didn't know she could be so much more than an actress, as if she was really in love herself with Ebony." Queel thought to himself. Queel had had Astyarress every which way it could come across in their minds over the years, the quiet storm has blown into one where deadly lightning could strike. Queel knew the time had come for his grand exit, a magician vanishing in a puff of smoke, leaving behind a legacy soaked in lust and deception.

But the true question remained, buried deep within the abyss of his soul. Queel's perspective left him questioning. Would his Machiavellian machinations lead to riches untold, or would they crumble beneath the weight of their own wickedness which even he was amazed at how far things had progressed especially for Astyarress who now was on the face of a major brand. Only the fickle hands of fate held the answer.

Pharaoh had shut down the video footage and Queel was only yet to feel the sting of this scorpion, he'd had only been given an introduction. This was not the last time Pharaoh's security would surface.

But before he'd end this last dance with Astyarress, he found himself drifting back to when they first met.

Chapter Two

So The Storm Begins

Once upon a time in a bustling city, there stood a unique and unconventional art studio that

catered to the expressive world of nude modeling. The studio was known for its avant-garde

approach, providing a platform for individuals to embrace and celebrate the beauty of their

naked form. This was a place where the boundaries were pushed, and inhibitions were left at

the door.

On a particularly revolutionary day, the ice was broken on introductions as two individuals

eagerly awaited the arrival of an artist who would capture their anatomical assets in all their

glory. Astyarress was this sexy, long legged, toned, raw and raspy voiced woman that caught his

eye, someone who had the same ambition he soon found out as their eyes met and never let go.

In this intimate setting, conversations flowed freely as the prospective nude bodies found solace

in each other's presence.

Queel, a charismatic and confident soul, had his eyes set on Astyarress, a breathtaking being

who radiated grace and charm

Once Queel and Astyarress caught each other's eyes they seemed to spin in the middle of the room, a crowded room of aspiring dirty dancers. Nude models, doing the dirty, metaphorically dancing amongst each other, looking and comparing themselves to one another but a quiet crowd. The models appeared to be observing just as much as the artist. Or so it seemed.

The tango would developed even more between the sheets. Queel walked up to Astyarress, wrapping his arm around Astyarress's nude waist, he ran his eyes from her mouth, to her lips that seemed to quiet their thoughts, he continued deeper into more body language. Queel ran his eyes from Astyarress's mouth tracing her frame from her neck down her anterior of her naked body. His penis couldn't help but become visibly erect in front of Astyarress. He continued his observation downward passing up the opportunity to touch the full, bare breasts in front him with a mischievous glance up towards Astyarress's eyes, wetting his bottom lip with his tongue as he was preparing to say something, he continued giving Astyarress a swirl outward from him, spinning her in a circle looking at her assets. Queel lightly smacked Astyarress on her ass, which he found to be firm but enough for him to linger with a little cusp of his hand as he looked into Astyarress face. "You look like you've put in a little work here and there", Queel said, smiling as he grinned, appreciating what he was looking at. Astyarress returned the touch by placing her hand on Queel's penis. with a slight flirtation stroke she ended with a bit of a grip test. "Firm, you shouldn't let that go to waste" said Astyarress. Queel looked away from Astyarress for a moment to see if anyone was paying attention to the beginnings of their tongues dancing back and forth with some hushed, flirting in front of everyone else.

"You sound like you might be interested" said Queel. Queel continued "Why might you be interested in poising as a nude model here?" Queel considered himself a little classy when it came to looking for prey, a chic to bone. After all he could continue grooming his artistic eye while looking fora gorgeous playmate. He thought to himself that today might be the day he would find one, given how forward Astyarress had returned the mild tap his delivered on her ass.

Astyarress replied "I'm trying to build my portfolio and overcome some inhibitions still haunting me." Queel had been erect and he found himself irresistible so he behaved as maturely as he could in handling his thoughts in accord with a room full of other naked people.

Queel leaned in towards Astyarress and asked her to accompany him back into the locker room which was a little ways from the main studio set As Queel and Astyarress walked towards the locker room, they left behind the bright lights and eyes of the main studio set. The locker room was dimly lit, with the only light coming from outside, where heavy rain was pouring down. Queel couldn't help but be drawn to the ethereal ambiance surrounding them. Large pane windows let in the thundering touch of raindrops, creating a symphony of nature's serenade.

The sounds of the studio were replaced by the soft pitter-patter of raindrops and the occasional roll of thunder.

The locker room was filled with rows of clothes hanging from hooks on the walls, creating a sense of seclusion and privacy. The air was cool and damp, with the faint scents, of moisture, perfumes from the fabrics filling the room.

They reached an opening near a large window pane, where the rain was pounding against the glass, distorting the view of the outside world but illuminating enough light on two naked bodies. Queel turned to face Astyarress, his eyes admiring her beauty in the dim light.

Astyarress too gazed at Queel, appreciating his strong physique, yet gentle presence. The moment was intimate and romantic, with the secluded atmosphere of the locker room and the sound of rain creating a sense of privacy and closeness. They stood there in silence for a moment, simply enjoying each other's company and the tranquility of the moment. The quiet was broken only by the soft sounds of their breathing and the occasional rustle of clothing as they moved closer to each other. The intimacy of the moment was heightened by the darkness and the sound of rain.

Queel again looked Astyarress up and down admirably, but gave no more verbal compliments at that moment. Astyarress too liked what she saw in front of her.

Queel asked Astyarress to come closer to him and stand in front of him as he began to speak. This was the origin of his pimp game he was about to run on Astyarress. "Maybe I can help you overcome some of your inhibitions", as he ran his fingers behind Astyarress's long hair which was cascading just above her ass in a ponytail that she had began to take down.

As Queel gently touched Astyarress's breast with his fingertips, the gesture sent a shiver of excitement through her body. He watched intently as his fingers moved slowly across her nipple, the contact sending sparks of pleasure through her skin.

Astyarress's breathing quickened as she anticipated Queel's next move. He leaned in closer, as if drawn in by her beauty and her presence.

His head followed his fingers, and he spoke softly and seductively making a symphony between his body language, his admiration and words, "Nice, real nice."

Astyarress's heart raced as Queel seemed about to continue his exploration of her body, but he suddenly cleared his throat and leaned back against the wall below the large window pane. The shift in his demeanor added a layer of tension and anticipation to the moment.

As he leaned back, Queel asked, "Did you have them done?" referring to Astyarress's breasts. Queel was referring to Astyarress' breast. There was a certain intimacy in his tone that suggested he was genuinely curious.

Astyarress had anticipated more from him in so far as touching but she wasn't thirsty enough

to have been disappointed that he hadn't continued making her insides melt or beginning more

of some kinda physical foreplay just yet. Actually he had but Astyarress was a bit behind

His question was blunt and direct, and yet, there was a certain intimacy in his tone that

suggested he was genuinely curious.

The air between them was thick with sexual tension as they stood there, inches apart, their

gazes locked on each other

Astyarress was standing directly in front of Queel naked waiting to see if it was going to be

worth her missing her opportunity to have been the object of the next masterpiece of art for

the modeling class amongst the other nude models.

Astyarress spoke "I'm listening, how exactly might you help me overcome my inhibitions?"

Queel replied, "haven't I already begun? I got you to follow a strange man into a dark, barely lit

room where the rain is overshadowing our voices, maybe even sounds, if things become a little

more interesting."

Astyarress replied " I think I might like to get to know you Queel, you're interesting. Will you be returning to the class?

Queel replied "Not just yet" as he pulled Astyarress in towards him, positioning her to straddle his legs with her long legs for only a moment. Then in an instance,

Queel picked Astyarress up wrapping those long legs around his torso and his arms under those long legs cuffing her backbone and buttocks in his arms. Queel spoke as serious as he could and told Astyarress he had a proposition for her but they could talk about all that later. Queel told Astyarress, "You're a little heavier than I anticipated" as he lifted her just a little higher off of his torso then teasingly setting her back down against him. You better slow up on the chow" in a joking way as he grabbed her ass and pulled her pelvis into him a little bit more letting her know he was indeed feeling the idea of having sex with her, her thoughts to say the least.

Astyarress thought Queel was a little hard to read. Queel then admitted to his interest in as he said, "I wanna fuck you and here would be the most impromptu place, the moment and an unforgettable introduction but" he said as he returned Astyarress's legs back to the floor.

Astyarress looked at him as in a little bit of disappointment.

Queel continued in a slow, quiet tone, real sly. "Yeah..., fucking you right here and now would open the next chapter wouldn't it?" Astyarress tried not to smile and replied "You think we might spend enough time with one another to write a book?"

Queel replied, as he again looked Astyarress up and down, nice and slow

"Yes Astyarress, but I do value your worth and mine. It's principles maybe..."

but before he could finish,

Astyarress kinda spoke sarcastically and said "Or maybe your sex game might not be as firm as the package leads on. Or you're getting enough sex at home?"

Queel replied "No Astyarress, my playboy days came to a hault not too long ago.

Getting pussy has never been a problem.

As for at home, I'm very much single.

But let me ask you something?

Based on my observations and the way you opened up to me…

your pussy all on me and shit, it didn't seem as if you would've minded if I was single or not?

What's that about? Wait, don't answer I kinda like my new cologne. It's called You."

Queel smiled at Astyarress.

Astyarress liked it and replied just above the tone of a whisper, "I won't."

Queel had shut it down and Astyarress was none the least impressed with their little move into seclusion to talk privately but bare ass naked, and no sex happened.

Astyarress said "You did end up wasting it" referring to Queel's penis as she made it obvious that she was looking at it.

"Nah" said Queel "You'll see what that's all about later. I suppose. If you're still game?

Queel was confident and he found Astyarress to be confident as well.

Then the real test happened as Queel and Astyarress were just about to leave the locker room and return back to the studio. Queel grabbed Astyarress hand gently and turned her towards him as he gave her another serious look. "You were interested in getting paid for this nude modeling gig right? You knew it wasn't entirely free right? That tells me you don't have any problem taking off your clothes for money if you don't mind me being blunt about it."

Astyarress was still a little hot from all the flirting. "No" she said, "I don't have a problem with that. I love my body." said Astyarress.

"And you should" replied Queel smiling again and surveying Astyarress's assets. How about pornography? Astyarress was stunned and surprised at how Queel was being straight forward with her about sex and not with him but the idea of having sex with another man.

Astyarress had to clear that up with a question,

 "You're talking about us? Or with another man? Or some type of Ménage à trois? It's sound like you're a freak Queel. You want to have sex with me and another woman for money or videotape us?"

Queel had turned away from Astyarress waiting for her to answer him, then he said, "I might want that. Would it or does that offend you?" said Queel.

Astyarress had gotten dickmitized from looking at his penis and the little bit of playfulness they had had already.

Astyarress replied "No. I'm not offended. As you can see, I'm a little more liberal than some women, I'm here right?"

Queel then turned around and sandwiched Astyarress between the door and his body then leaned in as if he were going to kiss Astyarress on those lips he'd been admiring ever since they met, Queel then said being as close to Astyarress, eye to eye, softly he whispered "I always ask. Can I?"

"Yes" said Astyarress hoping this time things would proceed a little more she had to admit to herself. Queel began kissing Astyarress passionately pressing her body into the door. Astyarress was impressed (and horny as ever now) by Queel. Queel backed off then stepped back, erect and wiped his chin using the inside of his hand, bringing his hand down as if he'd tasted as that he was looking at but proceeded only with his eyes to continue the seduction. Astyarress smiled.

Queel said , "I think we better get in there, that is if we're going to catch the last part of this session. That is if you're going to stay longer?"

Astyarress asked "So you can turn it on and off just like that? I just knew we were getting ready to fuck this time."

Queel smiled and opened the door a little bit with some last words and questions. "After you Astyarress.

Is Astyarress your real name or just for this nude modeling, so no one's in your business?"

Queel was remembering all the details as to how the two of them started their acquaintance and how intrigued he had been with Astyarress when they first met. How he had began grooming Astyarress first hand earlier on.

Queel had been serious from his introduction with Astyarress about investing some time with her into pursuing pornography, starting with him. Astyarress too had felt not only a curiosity about the idea but she wanted to pursue some time being spent with Queel.

Chapter Three

The Audition

Stroking the canvas of his grand plan, Queel had shared his aspirations with Astyarress, who

found herself irresistibly intrigued. She, too, wanted to broaden the horizons of their union.

The promise of a future call, had left Astyarress intrigued and excited. True to his word, the

call came, but it was no ordinary conversation; it was an audition for something beyond their

wildest dreams. Meeting at Queel's loft, Astyarress was greeted by an air of confidence that

matched her own. Queel sensed her big ego and admired it, recognizing the power it held

alongside her unwavering self-assurance. As the night unfolded, the couple found themselves

indulging in a sumptuous feast, of passionate conversations and shared laughter. The safe

haven of Queel's contemporary loft, is where their desire grew, transforming the evening into

an enchanting and intimate audition in getting past the unspoken words and into bed with one

another. Queel, never one to shy away from directness, encouraged Astyarress to showcase her

talents, both in and out of the bedroom with him. Their steps were taken slowly, each move

was filled with anticipation, like a playful game of twister. This was a foreplay unlike any other

that Astyarress had had, it was wherein the boundaries of pleasure melded seamlessly with exploration. In the midst of their sensual dance, Queel revealed a new dimension to their connection. He expressed not only a desire for private moments but also an invitation for Astyarress to explore the world of pornography as a duo, exploiting the opportunities recently presented to him as a photographer. The flame of curiosity flickered within her as she contemplated the limitless possibilities this partnership held.

The night continued its gentle symphony as their bodies intertwined in a passionate embrace. The warmth of Queel's bedroom fireplace lulled them into an embrace of intimacy where the two of them made their way to the floor during sex.

They reveled in the connection they had found and knew that this was merely the beginning of their journey together.

And so, as the night drew to a close.

Queel and Astyarress had discovered not only passion but also a shared hunger for exploration and growth. With the slumber of satisfaction blanketing their bodies, they closed their eyes, knowing that their journey had only just begun.

Listening in silence
I came to watch
I remain in tacked
As you slow down everything
Just for the crowd of one tonight
I'm pushing through the silent wave
The crowd around you
Waiting
To speak explicitly to you
I came to touch
I remain in lust
Tonight
I came to ...
Now slow down everything
Just for us
Just for tonight
No tickets
No air
I came to loosen my collar, loosen my hair
To happen upon.
Things explicitly
As I recall
As I was listening in silence
I heard
You wanted this
You wanted me
I came
Now I'm here Tonight
As you slow down everything
Could you recall
Just for us
Recall explicitly
Tongues

I came to...
Loosen my collar
Loosen and happen upon things
Should you happen
To get explicit
Explicitly with you
I came to touch
Later
I want you to recall, to watch
For the crowd of one
Tonight
Just for us
We can slow this down
To leave things
Explicit tongues between us

Chapter 4

The Invitation

Queel decided to have Astyarress come back to his loft where they could further their discussion on a particular topic and if she'd forgotten he'd like to refresh her memory, possibly lessen the bit of amnesia if that was the case.

Queel opens the conversation.

Queel: (Grinning) Well well, Astyarress, looks like our discussion will continue at my loft this weekend if you'd like a second date. I hope you haven't forgotten the topic we were exploring last time. Or maybe you've encountered some selective memory loss over the past week?

Astyarress: (Laughs) Oh, Queel, I assure you my memory is intact. Although, I must admit, your playful teasing is a bit concerning. Memory loss? That's an interesting way to invite me back to your place.

Queel: (Grinning mischievously) "Can't blame a guy for trying to be memorable, can you? But seriously, I did enjoy our last conversation, and I'm eager to continue exploring the topic with you. Plus, I'll make sure to review anything you might have forgotten. Maybe I have some special technique for memory enhancement hidden up my sleeve."

Astyarress: (Playfully rolling her eyes) "Oh, I can only imagine the innovative methods you've come up with for memory recovery, Queel. Well, I'm game. Let's see if your secret techniques can truly erase any memory loss I might have encountered this past week"

Queel: (Laughing) "I like the sound of that. But fear not, Astyarress, your memory is safe with me. And if it turns out I do have a method for reversing memory loss, you'll be the first to know."

Astyarress: (Teasingly) "Should I be concerned about this "secret method" of yours? Who knows what kind of memories will resurface if I let you experiment on me?"

Queel: (Feigning innocence) "Oh, never fear, Astyarress! My secret method is completely safe, I promise. No repressed memories or anything like that. Just a good old-fashioned memory refresher session as we continue our discussion."

Astyarress: (Smiling) "Well, in that case, I suppose I'll have to trust you and your secret method. Lead the way, Secret Agent Queel. Let's continue our exploration of that intriguing topic, without any memory distractions, of course.

Queel: (Offering his arm) Your trust is well-placed, my dear Astyarress. Together, we shall uncover the mysteries of this topic and ensure that memory loss never hinders our conversations. I'll see you soon"

Once Astyarress arrives it's not too long before Queel embarks on the topic of discussion.

Queel: "Astyarress, I have something on my mind that I must share with you. It's about our connection and how I believe we can take it to an entirely new dimension."

Astyarress: "Oh, Queel, you've piqued my curiosity. Pray, do share what you have in mind."

Queel: "Well, recently, I've discovered incredible opportunities as a pornography. And it occurred to me that we could explore the world of pornography together, in a more intimate and personal way. Think about it, Astyarress, the potential is limitless. We could create beautiful and private moments that are unique to our connection, capturing them through the lens."

Astyarress: (surprised) "Queel, I must admit, this suggestion took me aback. It's not something I had ever envisioned exploring. But... I can't deny the flame of curiosity flickering within me. What do you see as the benefits of such a partnership?"

Queel: "Ah, Astyarress, I knew the idea might come as a surprise. But, imagine the freedom we would have in expressing our desires and exploring our sensuality. Through the art of photography, we could create a safe and judgment-free space to explore ourselves and each other. Plus, the impact we could make by showcasing the beauty and authenticity of our connection to the world is truly exciting."

Astyarress: (thoughtful) "I see your point, Queel. It's true that the realm of pornography often carries a negative connotation, but perhaps we could change that. By showcasing our genuine connection and expressing our desires freely, we could offer the world an alternative perspective – one that celebrates intimacy and openness."

Queel: "Exactly, Astyarress. Our partnership could challenge societal norms and expectations. We can show the world that pornography doesn't have to be solely about objectification, but rather a platform for genuine human connection and exploration."

Astyarress: (softly) "Queel, I find myself intrigued by your proposal. This venture would require trust, open communication, and a shared vision. But if we can navigate those hurdles, I believe we could create something truly meaningful."

Queel: "I knew you would understand, Astyarress. Together, we can establish boundaries, ensuring that our private moments remain sacred and cherished. It's vital that we approach this with respect for ourselves and our connection. It's not just about the art of pornography, but also about understanding and embracing our desires."

Astyarress: "I agree, Queel. This exploration will require introspection and self-awareness. We must always prioritize our emotional well-being and ensure that our partnership remains strong throughout this creative process."

Queel: "Precisely, Astyarress. Our connection is the foundation of all we do. So, if at any point either of us feels uncomfortable or uneasy, we will communicate honestly and without judgment."

Astyarress: "Thank you, Queel, for your thoughtfulness and understanding. I'm willing to embark on this journey with you. Let's delve into this realm of possibility together and see where our dual exploration takes us."

Queel: "Astyarress, your willingness reassures me greatly. I believe our partnership holds boundless potential, both creatively and personally. Let's embrace this new dimension and create something extraordinary, leaving no stone unturned in our exploration."

Together: "Let our curiosity guide us, and may our connection shine through every frame we capture."

The conversation gets a little more intimate before Queel says

"Shall we eat?"

It's the appetite of a rush

The taste and bittersweet

The skintight dew

that warms me

When you're gone

bittersweet remains

The appetite within

I taste and eat

The bittersweet

It's the rush

I find calling inside

Inside the warmth and chill of

this skintight dew

The appetite for you

And when your gone

The last drop

The last drop I'll savor

Like a pea

The smallest piece not leaving none, none for you, just my appetite

Just my appetite within

The rush I find calling inside quieted by the sheep of truth, the warmth and chill of skintight dew.

They pushed boundaries and explored every inch of their desires, relinquishing themselves towards exploration and giving themselves fully to the trios: the intoxication of passion enveloping right now at this moment, for the intoxication of money, wealth, material things but also for Queel he wanted a name for himself. Astyarress did not despute Queel's intelligence and considered him a worthy partner. The next several weeks turned into years bringing new challenges, of course initiated by Queel, but there was money resulting from following and collaborating with Queel. All Queel had to do was learn what motivated Astyarress, her needs intimately and assure her he wasn't committing himself to anyone else as a full time lover. He expected the same.

After Sunset

The sands of the hour fall, the sands of time answering the dawn's nakedness the hours unveiled breathlessly time spent with you, thoughts that caress ring into the next, sunset befalls from the sands of the hour, these are the sands of time …enclosing the next sunset repeating the hour, sunset's ray kisses the pale night, the moon chariots across the cumulus pillowing the moon, as I lay my head in its shadow red as the dawn, in blows the red sheer of an open glass door until it touches the shoulder of the hour as the kiss that first caressed once again welcoming the dawn, sands of the hour fall to tell of kisses that close the sunset, Dawn caresses me after your kisses have closed the sunset Jocelyn Shaw

#009/Sunset Kisses

Dawn caresses me after your kisses have closed the sunset, sands of the hour fall until I hear your voice, slowly the color fades the dawn with reminisces of the time spent with you, an arrow of cupid misrayed my way the day I met you, so unexpected as the thoughts that caress, fall from the sands of the hour, as this unexpected note of love sent your way, a message in a bottle, an old romantic gesture, floating, float on, until notes of your voice ring my way, unexpectedly, the sands of the hour fall, the sands of time Jocelyn Shaw

Chapter Five

We Gotta Go Back

Queel had remained focused on his career. He was ambitious, constantly seeking opportunities to showcase his talent and prove himself. He is not afraid to take risks and experiment with unconventional photography techniques, which often leads to stunning results. It was Queel's presentation that had impressed Lotus and Emystary who recognized Queel's talent in some photos Emystary had reviewed before hiring an intern. Queel had unique style and ability to connect with his subjects, making his photographs captivating and evocative.Queel's statement which accompanied his portfolio is what stood out. A statement which would come to frutrition. In his one paragraph introduction he made it visibly reassuring that he believed that every photograph he takes should tell a story, capturing the essence of both the subject and the photographer's vision. Queel is in his late 20s, with a charismatic personality that drew the attention of Lotus who conferred his thoughts to Emystary. Queel was a professional indeed,, when it cams to his work.one of the best Emystary had been in contract with at her studio. While his reputation had preceded him, his talent and dedication surpassed his title as an intern at the studio where he had been earning respect in the competitive world of photography.

Queel secretly maintaining a relationship with Astyarress throughout his internship only

decided to take a risk later involving Astyarress after he accidentally ome across some

paperwork including bank statements and ledgers Lotus had left in his office whereas he

trusted Queel to close up the studio after he'd left for the day. It was all attractive to Queel to

say the least. It was then the gears in Queel's mind tinkered with the idea of becoming more of

a figure around the studio but he would have to be crafty and loosen his grip on Astyarress.

Queel had trusted Astyarress for she'd gone along with all of Queel's ideas in the past.Queel

knew that he had to be secretive in implementing his blueprint at the studio. Queel

meticulously calculated studio schedules, clients, and the perfect moment to take a shot at

introducing Astyarress.who was a damn good actress, skilled in seduction, and without a doubt

beautiful as any of the other models that had came through the studio doors. He didn't want

to risk his reputation or jeopardize his internship, so he devised a plan that was astute and

deliberate. A plan that was ever so cunning which ultimately be in need of Astyarress's

confidence and charm to persuade Ebony into an affair. Astyarress would be his pawn only to

lure Ebony closer to them, while also convincing Astyarress that there would be a significant

payoff bigger than ever to secure her pockets without wasting her time. Lastly, Astyarress

would be giving up her place in the bed regularly with Queel, who in a way had became her

security blanket although she'd come into their Bonnie and Clyde hustles as a strong, confident woman. Queel needed that confidence to convince Ebony to have an affair with her.

In the beginning, Queel started by subtly suggesting ideas to Astyarress during their private meetings. He strategically planted seeds of influence, making her believe that the ideas were actually her own. She owned it, not him. She would be the legs of the spider weaving this web. He would praise her creativity and make her feel valued, all while slowly guiding her towards his own vision.

Queel also began to undermine Lotus behind the scenes. He knew that Lotus had a weakness for flattery, so he used his charm and charisma to gain his trust. Queel would casually drop compliments about Lotus's work in conversations, always making sure that it reached his ears. This not only boosted Lotus's ego but also made him more inclined to listen to Queel's opinions. Trust. Commitment. Loyalty. As Queel's reputation continued to grow within the studio, he started taking more risks with his photography. He didn't shy away from pushing boundaries or experimenting with more unconventional techniques. His stunning and mesmerizing photographs started to gain attention not only from his colleagues but also from prospective clients abroad. The more successful Queel became in securing trust of Lotus, the more power he felt inside. He started subtly persuading Lotus to implement his ideas and suggestions, always couching them in terms of achieving greater success for the studio. Such as campaigning just far enough from Emystary to start some intimate plays behind the scenes. Queel fed off the excitement and admiration he received from his colleagues, people who were including him in their inner circle. The keys of friendship. or so they thought. Queel was relishing in the knowledge that his sneaky maneuvers were leading him closer to his ultimate goal.

But Queel knew that he had to remain vigilant and maintain the delicate balance between his relationship with Astyarress keeping her in check, and continued manipulation of Astyarress. He understood that he couldn't let either of them discover his true intentions, for it would be the end of his carefully crafted plan.

In his late-night rendezvous with Astyarress, Queel would assure her of his commitment and devotion, planting the seeds that she was a rue talent in pulling this off without any history to support her as a model and being seen by everyone as apart of Emystary and Ebony's reputable services and professional talents.He would subtly hint at opportunities where the possibilities could become more apparent, she could shine brighter, but he was always careful not to arouse her suspicions that this was not going to be anything less than them as cohorts, him having her

back.

As time went by, Queel became more confident in his abilities and his ability to manipulate

those around him. His talent and ambition were paying off, and he could taste the sweet

victory that lay just within his reach.

Queel had transformed from a talented yet unnoticed intern into a master of manipulation.

He had delicately woven his way through the studio, silently pulling the strings and bending

everyone to his will. And as he continued to rise to the top, he couldn't help but revel in his

own brilliance.

Chapter Six

Friendship

Ebony was seething in his office, a whirlwind of anger, confusion, and anguish tearing through him. The disturbing conversation he'd with Pharaoh reminded Ebony about what was in the video feed, as to where he had collected spy cams in their rooms, and how revealing a twisted dilemma this was that demanded their immediate attention. They couldn't afford to be passive. They couldn't sit idle while this chaos consumed them.

Pharaoh had finally arrived to meet Ebony in person. Ebony, told Pharaoh "I'm glad you're here," There was a jumble of emotions palpable behind his words. "This situation with Queel has spiraled out of control, and if we want to have any chance of returning the favor to Astyarress not being alerted, we need to obliterate this problem from both our lives." Pharaoh then tells Ebony "You know I could have utilized my resources without coming in person, but I wanted to join you in person to have a more personalized discussion with an old friend. After all, it's been a long time since we had a chance to catch up on what direction our lives went since we last did this". Ebony with his frustration barely contained replied "I know," Although he couldn't help, show the intensity of his anger reverberating in the air.

Pharaoh wasted no time, urgently instructing Ebony, "We have to move swiftly and with precision. Our first task is to secure the evidence. We cannot allow Queel to use it as a tool for blackmail or further manipulation."

"You're damn right, One thing is undeniably true. Queel managed to deceive everyone for sometime, said Ebony with a voice filled with sharpness and determination, his eyes burning with seething resentment.

Pharaoh, sensing Ebony's fiery rage, assured him, "I've already mobilized my security team. But we must handle this video footage with extreme caution, shielding it from prying eyes and malicious intentions.

"We cannot allow Queel to get away with this treachery! If he thinks he can hold anything over us, he's dead wrong. I want that evidence locked away so securely that not even the gods themselves could find it!"

Ebony clenched his fists, expressing his fury. The sheer audacity of Queel, using their vulnerabilities against them, fueled a burning fury within him." He underestimated us,

Pharaoh. But mark my words, he will pay for his role in the deceit behind Astyarress'

performance, no less invading my privacy."

Pharaoh's face twisted into a snarl as he pounded his fist against the table.

"The legacy that you and Emystary have built. Pathetic! I feel your anger and confusion as to

how and why the two of them Queel and Astyarress would portray day to day, week after week,

home and abroad their commitment. Hadn't they received lucrative opportunities?" Pharaoh

continued.

Ebony: "We can't afford to be passive in this, Pharaoh. We must take action now."

Pharaoh: "Queel and Astyarress deserve nothing less than our ruthless retaliation, they'll regret

everything that has come to past."

Ebony: "We will make them pay for their treachery, yet be as cunning as Queel and Astyarress."

Pharaoh: "Yes, Ebony! Let them taste the bitter fruit of their betrayal. We shall unleash a storm

upon them, a storm that will leave them nothing. After all this time and how you supported his

career."

Ebony: "The corruption of greed which consumed Queel will be his downfall, Pharaoh."

Pharaoh: "Our legacy is behind us, once again together, there will be triumph and justice,

Ebony.

Ebony: "Precision".

Pharaoh: "We will be the relentless, the architects of their demise."

Ebony: "Leave no stone unturned, no bounds, Pharaoh. Together, we can do this."

Pharaoh: "Indeed, Ebony. Our wrath will be swift and merciless. Queel and Astyarress will

regret the day they ever crossed our path. Prepare yourself, my friend, for the storm is coming,

and we shall be its masters."

Together, united by an inferno of anger, Pharaoh and Ebony set forth to retrieve the evidence,

without a confrontation with Queel.

As they solidified their agreement to secure the evidence, Pharaoh proposed their next move,

his voice tinged with exasperation. "This is going to cause damage, Ebony. We need to assess

the magnitude of it. I'm working hand in hand with my security team and risk management to evaluate the consequences this affair has already had on your reputation. If there's someone out there other than Queel who knows about your comings and goings. Only then can we develop a plan to minimize the fallout."

Ebony's exasperated sigh resonated through the room, his mind swirling with apprehension. "I can't afford a tarnished reputation or jeopardize my engagement with Emystary," he muttered bitterly. "Every step must be calculated, Pharaoh. We can't afford any missteps."

Pharaoh's nod was filled with understanding, his voice calm yet laced with urgency. "I understand, Ebony. But to tackle this scandal head-on, we need more information. I propose that I examine all the occasions when Astyarress was around while you were with Queel. It might shed light on Queel's motives and ruthless intentions."

The intensity of Ebony's anger simmered momentarily, replaced by a newfound determination. "That's a damn good idea, Pharaoh," he growled. "Connecting the dots could uncover vital clues and help us dismantle Queel's insidious plan."

Pharaoh, ever resilient, continued with purpose. "Once we have a clearer picture, we must prepare for a confrontation. We'll need to strategize on how best to face Queel. It might be wise to involve legal counsel, ensuring we navigate within the boundaries of the law."

Ebony's heavy sigh weighed him down, the enormity of the situation crushing his spirit. "Yes, so be it. We'll do whatever it takes to protect ourselves legally. And Pharaoh, we must keep this sordid mess under wraps. Utmost discretion is paramount. We can't risk further exposure or unnecessary attention."

Pharaoh's agreement was resolute, his voice firm. "Absolutely, Ebony. Absolute discretion and unwavering security are non-negotiable. Our conversations and actions must remain impervious to prying eyes."

The weight of their predicament settled heavily on Ebony's shoulders, yet dispear wasn't an emotion or characteristic of any of Ebony's attributes, he would continue as Pharaoh suggested, "Ebony, trust me on this. Seek guidance from my experience. I've battled enough scandals to offer valuable advice on navigating this treacherous terrain."

Ebony's relief was palpable, his gratitude overwhelming. "I need that guidance, Pharaoh. Your wisdom and support will be critical. We will make calculated decisions and untangle this convoluted mess, all while keeping Emystary in the dark. I can't wait to see how you enlighten Astyarress. We'll come to terms on where that ends. That is if you decide not keep her around. You think you can keep her in line this time?"

After all this anger he'd shed throughout their meeting up until now, Ebony's lips curled into a knowing smile, his voice dripping with confidence. "Astyarress was very quick to hide her hands, or rather her involvement with me," Ebony began, his sharp eyes never leaving Pharaoh's face. "Did she disclose anything further to you?"

Pharaoh leaned forward, intrigued by the sudden shift in tone.

Ebony chuckled, a glint of mischief in his eyes. "You must have filled her head with some ideas or left more than an invitation for her to consider, something must have sparked her interest in ways she couldn't resist." Ebony smiled. She wasn't her usual self, avoiding the paparazzi or inquisitive about my agenda," he mused, his mind connecting the dots. "She told me she'd gotten a last minute invitation but she couldn't proceed with the details only that she didn't know if it were going to be a couple days or weeks after her departure. She was so confident

that I would be too caught up in my own marital affairs to question her absence." I knew you,

Pharaoh you were who it was she was going to be with of course as we'd discussed. As a matter

of fact I'm sure she could account for my time very well. You might want to check her accounts

or her itinerary notations throughout the campaign to get an idea as to what exactly our little

accomplice has in her own agenda, and her reports Queel as if he needed any verbal assurance.

I'm sure they shared some conversations as to the directions in which there plans were taking

shape."

Ebony leaned back in his seat, a satisfied expression on his face. "Oh, Pharaoh, my friend," he

said, his voice laced with a mix of pride and amusement. "You've unknowingly stumbled upon

something much more intricate than you initially thought. Astyarress has proven herself to of

hidden talents, but with the right motivations, she can be bent to our will. Together, we can

ensure she stays in line and serves our greater purpose, of course the resolution of this affair

with Queel. Right?"

Pharaoh's lips rose into a smile as he thought about this beautiful woman, she was of more

than one face obviously. "Indeed, Ebony," he replied, his voice oozing with confidence. "Our little accomplice has just revealed more than she intended, and it's time we exploited it. Let's uncover the depths of her intentions and ensure that her loyalty shifts to me as she believes she'll be the new lover in my life. Or should I say my presence?”

Pharaoh and Ebony continued to debate, outlining a plan that prioritized their well-being and reputations. They were resolved to confront this demon with ferocity, no matter the cost. Nothing would stand in their path as they fought to protect their interests and put this agonizing turmoil to rest.

Pharaoh's smile mirrored Ebony's as he envisioned their retort.

"Oh yes, my friend," he replied, a mixture of sweet anticipation and unmitigated satisfaction could be heard in the tone of his voice as he turned to Ebony from looking out the window of the hotel penthouse suite.

 "Astyarress has no idea where this going to lead. I can just imagine her mind reeling, trying to process our little family secret."

Ebony couldn't help but let out a small chuckle, quickly composing himself to maintain a serious demeanor. "Shem." Ebony chuckled again at the joke of Pharaoh introducing Astyarress to his identical twin which surely was more than Astyarress anticipated.

"Seriously, it's not every day you come face-to-face with your own echo, is it?

And Shem, my dear twin sister, she's doing an excellent job keeping our new friend thoroughly occupied I'm sure. I can guarantee that Astyarress has been left utterly perplexed and stung by the brilliance of how much, much more there was in our introduction" said Pharaoh in a very serious tone.

www.ingramcontent.com/pod-product-compliance
Lightning Source LLC
Chambersburg PA
CBHW081200130726
47996CB00009B/3192